Skateboard Design and Construction
How Your Board Gets Built

Justin Hocking

The Rosen Publishing Group's
PowerKids Press™
New York

To Matt and Sean

Published in 2006 by The Rosen Publishing Group, Inc.
29 East 21st Street, New York, NY 10010

First Edition

Editors: Melissa Acevedo and Orli Zuravicky
Book Design: Elana Davidian

Special thanks to Nick Hartman and Brian Petrie.
Photo Credits: Cover, pp. 7, 8 (bottom left and right), 15 (bottom right), 16 (bottom left), 19-20 BLADES Board & Skate, 659 Broadway, New York, NY/ photos by Cindy Reiman; pp. 4, 8 (top), 16 (bottom right) Brian Petrie, President, Earthwing Skateboards www.earthwingskateboards.com/ photos by Nancy Optiz; pp. 11, 12 (insets), 13 (top and bottom right), 15 (top) © Ed J Szalajeski/ Icon SMI; p. 12 (right) PS Stix; p. 16 (top) © Rud-gr.com-zefa/Masterfile.

Library of Congress Cataloging-in-Publication Data

Hocking, Justin.
Skateboarding design and construction : how your board gets built / Justin Hocking.
   p. cm. — (Power skateboarding)
Includes bibliographical references and index.
ISBN 1-4042-3048-3 (library binding)
1. Skateboards—Design and construction—Juvenile literature. I. Title. II. Series.

TT174.5.S35H63 2006
685'.362—dc22

2004022496

Manufactured in the United States of America

Contents

Skateboard design and construction has really changed over the years! The skateboard on the top is from the 1960s. The skateboard in the middle is from the 1970s. The board on the bottom is from the 1980s. Notice how different the 1980s board looks from the others.

History of the Skateboard

People have been riding skateboards since they were invented in America during the 1940s. The first skateboards were built by kids. They took the wheels off their roller skates and nailed them to the bottoms of flat wooden **planks**. Soon thousands of kids took their skateboards to the streets in places like New York's Lower East Side and Santa Monica, California.

People soon recognized the need for skateboards. In 1963, the first skateboard manufacturing companies, Makaha and Hobie, were formed. They began **mass-producing** skateboards. Over the years skateboard **design** has gone through changes to allow skaters to be more imaginative. In 1971, the **kicktail** was invented, which made turning easier. In the 1980s, the boards became wider and had a short **nose** and a long tail.

Most of the skateboards in the 1970s were long and narrow, like the shape of a surfboard. They were sometimes called banana boards because of their shape.

Modern Skateboards

Skateboarding has changed a lot over the years, and the design of skateboards has changed, too. Today **street skating** is the most popular kind of skateboarding. Most modern street **decks** are between 7 and 8 inches (18–20 cm) wide and about 31 inches (79 cm) long. The nose and tail are both large and upturned. Modern boards are also **concave** from side to side. When something is concave, it curves up at the edges, like a spoon. A board that is slightly concave from side to side gives skaters more control with their feet and adds strength to the board.

Another modern addition is the use of **grip tape**. Grip tape is bumpy on one side and sticky on the other side. The grip tape is placed on the top of the deck to help the skater keep his or her feet from slipping off the board.

The picture above shows a finished board with grip tape. *Top inset:* A worker lays grip tape on the deck of a board. *Middle inset:* After laying the grip tape on the board, the worker cuts it to fit the board perfectly. *Bottom inset:* The worker drills holes through the grip tape.

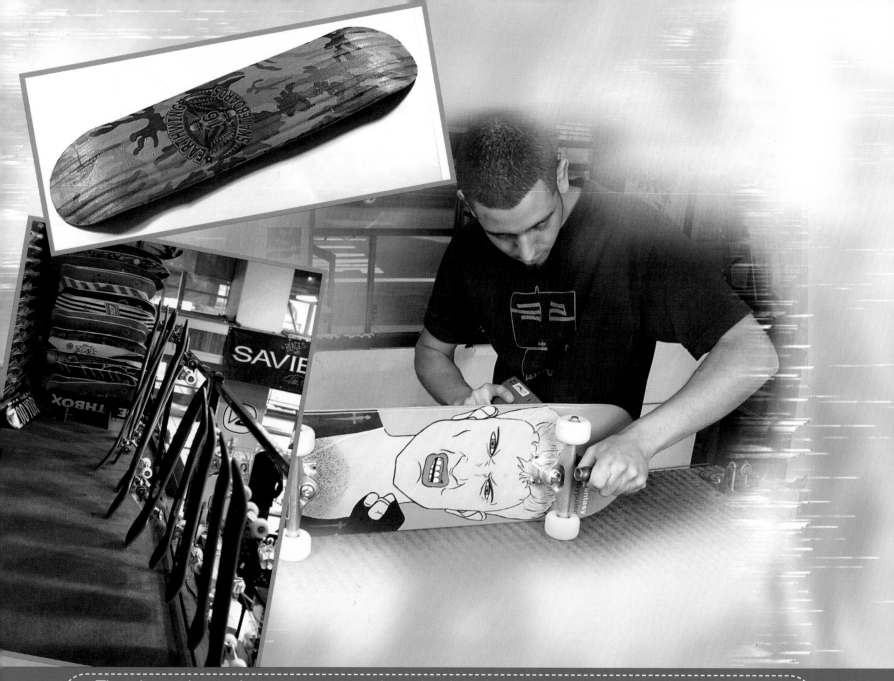

The photo above shows a man securing wheels to his finished board. *Top inset:* Earthwing Skateboards created this board using many different colors and graphics. *Bottom inset:* Skateboard shops have all kinds of skateboards for different styles of skaters.

Designing a Pro Board

There are many popular skateboard companies that do more than just create and sell skateboarding gear. In addition to making high-quality skateboard decks, many of these companies **sponsor** a team of **professional**, or pro, skaters. These pro skaters are paid to skateboard, and they also get to design their own "pro-model" skateboards.

When it is time for a pro to design a new skateboard, he or she usually meets with a company designer. Different pros ask for decks of different sizes and shapes, depending on their height, weight, shoe size, and the type of skating they do. Pros who street skate a lot use thinner boards, which makes **maneuvering** on street **obstacles** easier. Pros who skate in pools with steep walls want the increased security that a wider deck can provide. Pro riders also help choose artwork, also called **graphics**, for the bottom of their board.

Choosing Wood for the Deck

The earliest skateboards of the 1950s and the 1960s were made from one solid, thick plank of wood, usually pine or oak. These boards were heavy and hard to control. Manufacturers realized that decks needed to be thinner and lighter. Companies began making decks by layering thin sheets of wood on top of each other, instead of using one big, solid plank. These thin layers are called veneers.

Since skateboards are ridden on hard surfaces and obstacles, they are often thrown around and cut up. Manufacturers decided to stop using pine and oak and started using wood from the sugar maple tree. Sugar maple wood is one of the strongest, most **flexible** types of lumber. The flexible nature of the wood helps the skaters control the board and allows it to last longer.

Most lumber-producing maples used for skateboard wood are found on tree farms. These farms are located in the eastern and southeastern parts of the United States.

This worker at a skateboard manufacturing company places pieces of maple wood veneer in the machine that glues them together. *Inset:* This stack of maple wood veneer has already been glued together.

This machine pushes the veneers together to form a skate deck. *Top inset:* This machine, called a router, cuts the board to size. *Bottom inset:* After being pressed and cut to size, these decks are ready to be designed.

How Skate Decks Are Pressed and Shaped

The first step in creating a deck is to cut the lumber from a fully grown maple tree into very thin veneers. These veneers are then sent to a skateboard manufacturer. Most skateboards are made of seven layers of thin veneers. Glue is placed between each veneer, like a wooden sandwich. These "sandwiches" are then placed into a machine that will press the wood veneers and glue together. This process is called the seven-ply sandwich construction.

Once the board is pressed, a slow-cooling process helps make the final product sturdy and stiff. After the glue dries, the deck is placed in a cutting machine called a router. The router is a computerized saw that is **preprogrammed** to cut decks into the shape and size that each pro skater wants.

The machine that presses veneers together uses hundreds of pounds of weight and very high heat. It also presses an exact concave shape into each board.

Skateboard Graphics

Skateboards are not only fun to ride, but they are also works of art. Graphics appear on the bottoms of most decks. Many of the designers who create graphics for skateboards are also well-known skaters. This is yet another reason skateboarding is such an imaginative sport!

Screen printing is the method used to place graphics on a skateboard. Once designers and pro riders decide on a graphic, the shape of the graphic is cut out from the center of a screen. The screen used is like the kind found in a screen door. The screen is then placed on the bottom of the skate deck. Paint is applied to the screen and spread with a thin plastic tool, one color at a time. The screen is then removed, leaving a perfectly shaped picture on the board.

Professional skateboarder and artist Mark Gonzales is famous for his inventive and funny graphics. They now appear on Krooked Skateboards.

The worker is screening a design on the board. *Insets:* Skateboard manufacturers often put their company names on the boards they make, in addition to graphics. The board on the left is from Krooked Skateboards. The board on the right is from Barcelona.

Modern skateboard wheels are made of urethane plastic. *Left inset:* Smaller, harder wheels are used by skaters who want to do more tricks. *Right inset:* Clay wheels were used on boards from the 1960s. They provided a faster ride than metal wheels.

Skateboard Wheels

The first skateboard wheels were made of metal. Around 1959, manufacturers started making wheels from hardened clay. Clay wheels were faster than metal but still made for a bumpy ride. They also slipped on **cement** surfaces. Finally in the early 1970s, manufacturers discovered that they could make a better wheel from a type of plastic called **urethane**. Urethane wheels give skaters a faster, smoother ride. They also grip the cement surface much better than clay or metal wheels did.

All modern wheels are made from urethane, though not all skateboard wheels are the same. Wheels come in all different sizes. They are measured by diameter. This is the distance from the top of the wheel to the bottom of the wheel. Most wheels are between 50 and 70 millimeters (2–3 inches) in diameter.

The size of skateboard wheels is very important. Bigger, softer wheels give the skater a smoother, faster ride. Smaller, harder wheels make it easier to do tricks.

Bearings are among the smallest parts of a skateboard, but they are also among the most important. Bearings allow the skateboard wheels to spin quickly on the **axles**, also known as trucks. The first skateboard bearings were nothing more than a bunch of tiny metal balls, also called ball bearings. They fit in the space between the wheel and the truck. Luckily someone in the 1970s came up with the idea of sealing ball bearings inside a small, round metal case. Sealed bearings are much faster and easier to clean than regular ball bearings.

Modern sealed bearings are rated on an ABEC scale. The ABEC scale groups bearings according to their **accuracy** and by how long they last. The rating system includes grades 1, 3, 5, 7, and 9. Bearings that rate 1 on the ABEC scale are the lowest range. Bearings that rate 7 or higher are the fastest. They also last the longest.

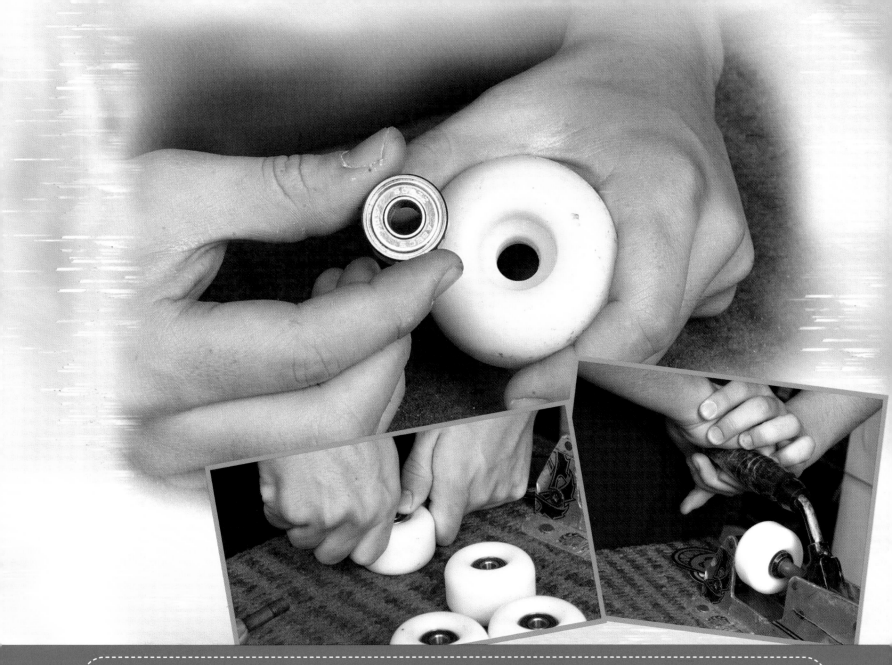

The picture above shows a bearing and the place into which it fits in the wheel. *Left inset:* A bearing is being put into a wheel. *Right inset:* A sealed bearing is being fixed to the wheel. Once the bearing has been placed in the wheel, the wheel can go on the skateboard.

There are many parts needed to make a skateboard, as shown above. *Left inset:* The axle is fixed to the board with small bolts, also called mounting hardware. *Right inset:* A small tool called a skate key is used to fix the wheel to the axle.

Skateboard Trucks

Trucks, or axles, are what fit the wheels to the skateboard and make it possible for them to turn. Trucks consist of several parts. The rectangular part of the truck is called the base plate. The top part of the truck is shaped like small bicycle handlebars. A large bolt called the kingpin connects the top of the truck to the base plate. The base plate is fixed to the base, or bottom, of the deck. The axle turns on two urethane cushions, also called **bushings**, as well as a third point on the base plate called the pivot cushion.

This truck design allows a skateboarder to turn simply by leaning in the direction she or he wants to go. A nut on the kingpin can be tightened or loosened to change the turning ability. Tighter trucks are harder to turn, but they make the board more solid. Loose trucks allow for easier turns and curves but can become unsteady at high speeds.

The seven-ply maple veneer skateboard has long been the standard in skateboard construction. Most companies have been uncertain about trying something new. Mervin Manufacturing, a company in Seattle, Washington, decided to experiment with different designs. They wanted to create a lighter, stronger, and faster skateboard. Instead of using maple wood for the deck of the board, this company used aspen wood. Aspen wood weighs less than maple wood and is just as strong. These boards have only three plies of wood instead of the usual seven. Because less wood and glue are used, the boards are lighter and faster. A maple wood skateboard is usually 3 pounds (1.4 kg). An aspen wood board weighs 2 pounds (1 kg). These skateboards have already sparked **competition** from other companies! As long as skaters ride skateboards, design and construction will continue to become better and better each year.

Glossary

accuracy (A-kyuh-ruh-see) The quality of being exactly right.

axles (AK-suhlz) Metal pieces that hold the wheels to the board and make it possible to turn.

bushings (BUSH-ingz) Shaped like small rubber O's, bushings fit on the kingpin and help the trucks turn smoothly.

cement (sih-MENT) A mixture of water, sand, and rock that hardens. It is often used for building.

competition (kom-pih-TIH-shin) A game or test.

concave (kon-KAYV) Dipping toward the center, like a spoon.

decks (DEKS) The wooden parts of skateboards that skaters stand on.

design (dih-ZYN) The plan or the form of something.

flexible (FLEK-sih-bul) Being able to move and bend in many ways.

graphics (GRA-fiks) Artwork that is screened onto the bottom of a skateboard.

grip tape (GRIP TAYP) Sticky on one side, bumpy on the other, grip tape is fixed to the top of the deck to prevent skaters from slipping off their boards.

kicktail (KIK-tayl) The rear part of the skateboard deck that slopes upward. A kicktail is also called a tail.

maneuvering (muh-NOO-ver-ing) Getting into or out of a position for a purpose.

mass-producing (mas-pruh-DOOS-ing) Making things in large amounts.

nose (NOHZ) The front part of a skateboard deck. The nose, like the tail, slopes upward.

obstacles (OB-stih-kulz) Any objects that can be used in a skateboarding trick.

planks (PLANKS) Thick, heavy wooden boards.

preprogrammed (pree-PROH-gramd) Planned to do something or have something done in advance.

professional (pruh-FEH-shuh-nul) Having to do with people who are paid for what they do.

sponsor (SPON-ser) To pay for an activity.

street skating (STREET SKAYT-ing) Skating in the street using obstacles, such as benches, stairs, and handrails.

urethane (YUR-ih-thayn) A special type of hard plastic used for making skateboard wheels.

Index

Web Sites

Due to the changing nature of Internet links, PowerKids Press has developed an online list of Web sites related to the subject of this book. This site is updated regularly. Please use this link to access the list: www.powerkidslinks.com/skate/design/